The Reservoir

JANET FRAME

A Phoenix Paperback

The Reservoir first appeared in *The New Yorker Magazine*
All stories taken from *The Reservoir & Other Stories*
published by W H Allen in 1966

This edition published in 1996 by Phoenix
a division of Orion Books Ltd
Orion House, 5 Upper St Martin's Lane, London WC2H 9EA

ISBN 1 85799 760 3

Typeset by Deltatype Ltd, Ellesmere Port, Cheshire
Printed in Great Britain by Clays Ltd, St Ives plc

CONTENTS

The Reservoir

It was said to be four or five miles along the gully, past orchards and farms, paddocks filled with cattle, sheep, wheat, gorse, and the squatters of the land who were the rabbits eating like modern sculpture into the hills, though how could we know anything of modern sculpture, we knew nothing but the Warrior in the main street with his wreaths of poppies on Anzac Day, the gnomes weeping in the Gardens because the seagulls perched on their green caps and showed no respect, and how important it was for birds, animals and people, especially children, to show respect!

And that is why for so long we obeyed the command of the grownups and never walked as far as the forbidden Reservoir, but were content to return 'tired but happy' (as we wrote in our school compositions), answering the question, Where did you walk today? with a suspicion of blackmail, 'Oh, nearly, nearly to the Reservoir!'

The Reservoir was the end of the world; beyond it, you fell; beyond it were paddocks of thorns, strange cattle, strange farms, legendary people whom we would never know or recognize even if they walked among us on a

Friday night downtown when we went to follow the boys and listen to the Salvation Army Band and buy a milk shake in the milk bar and then return home to find that everything was all right and safe, that our mother had not run away and caught the night train to the North Island, that our father had not shot himself with worrying over the bills, but had in fact been downtown himself and had bought the usual Friday night treat, a bag of licorice allsorts and a bag of chocolate roughs, from Woolworth's.

The Reservoir haunted our lives. We never knew one until we came to this town; we had used pump water. But here, in our new house, the water ran from the taps as soon as we turned them on, and if we were careless and left them on, our father would shout, as if the affair were his personal concern, 'Do you want the Reservoir to run dry?'

That frightened us. What should we do if the Reservoir ran dry? Would we die of thirst like Burke and Wills in the desert?

'The Reservoir,' our mother said, 'gives pure water, water safe to drink without boiling it.'

The water was in a different class, then, from the creek which flowed through the gully; yet the creek had its source in the Reservoir. Why had it not received the pampering attention of officialdom which strained weed and earth, cockabullies and trout and eels, from our tap water? Surely the Reservoir was not entirely pure?

'Oh no,' they said, when we inquired. We learned that the water from the Reservoir had been 'treated.' We supposed this to mean that during the night men in light-blue uniforms with sacks over their shoulders crept beyond the circle of pine trees which enclosed the Reservoir, and emptied the contents of the sacks into the water, to dissolve dead bodies and prevent the decay of teeth.

Then, at times, there would be news in the paper, discussed by my mother with the neighbors over the back fence. Children had been drowned in the Reservoir.

'No child,' the neighbor would say, 'ought to be allowed near the Reservoir.'

'I tell mine to keep strictly away,' my mother would reply.

And for so long we obeyed our mother's command, on our favorite walks along the gully simply following the untreated cast-off creek which we loved and which flowed day and night in our heads in all its detail – the wild sweet peas, boiled-lolly pink, and the mint growing along the banks; the exact spot in the water where the latest dead sheep could be found, and the stink of its bloated flesh and floating wool, an allowable earthy stink which we accepted with pleasant revulsion and which did not prompt the 'inky-pinky I smell Stinkie' rhyme which referred to offensive human beings only. We knew where the water was shallow and could be paddled in, where forts could be made from the rocks; we knew the frightening deep places where the eels lurked and the weeds were tangled in gruesome shapes; we knew the jumping places, the mossy stones with their dangers, limitations, and advantages; the sparkling places where the sun trickled beside the water, upon the stones; the bogs made by roaming cattle, trapping some of them to death; their gaunt telltale bones; the little valleys with their new growth of lush grass where the creek had 'changed its course,' and no longer flowed.

'The creek has changed its course,' our mother would say, in a tone which implied terror and a sense of strangeness, as if a tragedy had been enacted.

We knew the moods of the creek, its levels of low-flow, half-high-flow, high-flow which all seemed to relate to interference at its source – the Reservoir. If one morning the water turned the color of clay and crowds of bubbles were passengers on every suddenly swift wave hurrying by, we would look at one another and remark with the fatality and reverence which attends a visitation or prophecy,

'The creek's going on high-flow. They must be doing something at the Reservoir.'

By afternoon the creek would be on high-flow, turbulent, muddy, unable to be jumped across or paddled in or fished in, concealing beneath a swelling fluid darkness whatever evil which 'they,' the authorities, had decided to purge so swiftly and secretly from the Reservoir.

For so long, then, we obeyed our parents, and never walked as far as the Reservoir. Other things concerned us, other curiosities, fears, challenges. The school year ended. I got a prize, a large yellow book the color of cat's mess. Inside it were editions of newspapers, *The Worms' Weekly*, supposedly written by worms, snails, spiders. For the first part of the holidays we spent the time sitting in the long grass of our front lawn nibbling the stalks of shamrock and reading insect newspapers and relating their items to the lives of those living on our front lawn down among the summer-dry roots of the couch, tinkertailor, daisy, dandelion, shamrock, clover, and ordinary 'grass.' High summer came. The blowsy old red roses shed their petals to the regretful refrain uttered by our mother year after year at the same time, 'I should have made potpourri, I have a wonderful recipe for potpourri in Dr Chase's Book.'

Our mother never made the potpourri. She merely quarreled with our father over how to pronounce it.

The days became unbearably long and hot. Our Christmas presents were broken or too boring to care about. Celluloid dolls had loose arms and legs and rifts in their bright pink bodies; the invisible ink had poured itself out in secret messages; diaries frustrating in their smallness (two lines to a day) had been filled in for the whole of the coming year. . . . Days at the beach were tedious, with no room in the bathing sheds so that we were forced to undress in the common room downstairs with its floor patched with wet and trailed with footmarks and sand and its tiny barred window (which made me believe that I was living in the French Revolution).

Rumors circled the burning world. The sea was drying up, soon you could paddle or walk to Australia. Sharks had been seen swimming inside the breakwater; one shark attacked a little boy and bit off his you-know-what.

We swam. We wore bathing togs all day. We gave up cowboys and ranches; and baseball and sledding; and 'those games' where we mimicked grown-up life, loving and divorcing each other, kissing and slapping, taking secret paramours when our husband was working out of town. Everything exhausted us. Cracks appeared in the earth; the grass was bled yellow; the ground was littered with beetle sheels and snail shells; flies came in from the unofficial rubbish-dump at the back of the house; the twisting flypapers hung from the ceiling; a frantic buzzing filled the room as the flypapers became crowded. Even the cat put out her tiny tongue, panting in the heat.

We realized, and were glad, that school would soon reopen. What was school like? It seemed so long ago, it seemed as if we had never been to school, surely we had forgotten everything we had learned, how frightening, thrilling and strange it would all seem! Where would we go on the first day, who would teach us, what were the names of the new books?

Who would sit beside us, who would be our best friend?

The earth crackled in early-autumn haze and still the February sun dried the world; even at night the rusty sheet of roofing-iron outside by the cellar stayed warm, but with rows of sweat-marks on it; the days were still long, with night face to face with morning and almost nothing in-between but a snatch of turning sleep with the blankets on the floor and the windows wide open to moths with their bulging lamplit eyes moving through the dark and their grandfather bodies knocking, knocking upon the walls.

Day after day the sun still waited to pounce. We were tired, our skin itched, our sunburn had peeled and peeled again, the skin on our feet was hard, there was dust in our hair, our bodies clung with the salt of sea-bathing and sweat, the towels were harsh with salt.

School soon, we said again, and were glad; for lessons gave shade to rooms and corridors; cloakrooms were cold and sunless. Then, swiftly, suddenly, disease came to the town. Infantile Paralysis. Black headlines in the paper, listing the number of cases, the number of deaths. Children everywhere, out in the country, up north, down south, two streets away.

The schools did not reopen. Our lessons came by post, in smudged print on rough white paper; they seemed make-shift and false, they inspired distrust, they could not compete with the lure of the sun still shining, swelling, the world would go up in cinders, the days were too long, there was nothing to do, there was nothing to do; the lessons were dull; in the front room with the navy-blue blind half down the window and the tiny splits of light showing through, and the lesson papers sometimes covered with unexplained blots of ink as if the machine which had printed them had broken down or rebelled, the lessons were even more dull.

Ancient Egypt and the flooding of the Nile!

The Nile, when we possessed a creek of our own with individual flooding!

'Well let's go along the gully, along by the creek,' we   7 would say, tired with all these.

Then one day when our restlessness was at its height, when the flies buzzed like bees in the flypapers, and the warped wood of the house cracked its knuckles out of boredom, the need for something to do in the heat, we found once again the only solution to our unrest.

Someone said, 'What's the creek on?'

'Half-high flow.'

'Good.'

So we set out, in our bathing suits, and carrying switches of willow.

'Keep your sun hats on!' our mother called.

All right. We knew. Sunstroke when the sun clipped you over the back of the head, striking you flat on the ground. Sunstroke. Lightning. Even tidal waves were threatening us on this southern coast. The world was full of alarm.

'And don't go as far as the Reservoir!'

We dismissed the warning. There was enough to occupy us along the gully without our visiting the Reservoir. First, the couples. We liked to find a courting couple and follow them and when, as we knew they must do because they were tired or for other reasons, they found a place in the grass and lay down together, we liked to make jokes about them, amongst ourselves. 'Just wait for him to kiss her,' we would say. 'Watch. There. A beaut. Smack.'

Often we giggled and lingered even after the couple had observed us. We were waiting for them to do it. Every man and woman did it, we knew that for a fact. We speculated about technical details. Would he wear a frenchie? If he didn't wear a frenchie then she would start having a baby and be forced to get rid of it by drinking gin. Frenchies, by the way, were for sale in Woolworth's. Some said they were fingerstalls, but we knew they were frenchies and sometimes we would go downtown and into Woolworth's just to look at the frenchies for sale. We hung around the counter, sniggering. Sometimes we nearly died laughing, it was so funny.

After we tired of spying on the couples we would shout after them as we went our way.

> Pound, shillings and pence,
> a man fell over the fence,
> he fell on a lady,
> and squashed out a baby,
> pound, shillings and pence!

Sometimes a slight fear struck us – what if a man fell on us like that and squashed out a chain of babies?

Our other pastime along the gully was robbing the orchards, but this summer day the apples were small green hard and hidden by leaves. There were no couples either. We had the gully to ourselves. We followed the creek, whacking our sticks, gossiping and singing, but we stopped, immediately silent, when someone – sister or brother – said, 'Let's go to the Reservoir!'

A feeling of dread seized us. We knew, as surely as we knew our names and our address Thirty-three Stour Street

Ohau Otago South Island New Zealand Southern Hemisphere The World, that we would some day visit the Reservoir, but the time seemed almost as far away as leaving school, getting a job, marrying.

And then there was the agony of deciding the right time – how did one decide these things?

'We've been told not to, you know,' one of us said timidly.

That was me. Eating bread and syrup for tea had made my hair red, my skin too, so that I blushed easily, and the grownups guessed if I told a lie.

'It's a long way,' said my little sister.

'Coward!'

But it *was* a long way, and perhaps it would take all day and night, perhaps we would have to sleep there among the pine trees with the owls hooting and the old needle-filled warrens which now reached to the center of the earth where pools of molten lead bubbled, waiting to seize us if we tripped, and then there was the crying sound made by the trees, a sound of speech at its loneliest level where the meaning is felt but never explained, and it goes on and on in a kind of despair, trying to reach a point of understanding.

We knew that pine trees spoke in this way. We were lonely listening to them because we knew we could never help them to say it, whatever they were trying to say, for if the wind who was so close to them could not help them, how could we?

Oh no, we could not spend the night at the Reservoir

among the pine trees.

'Billy Whittaker and his gang have been to the Reservoir, Billy Whittaker and the Green Feather gang, one afternoon.'

'Did he say what it was like?'

'No, he never said.'

'He's been in an iron lung.'

That was true. Only a day or two ago our mother had been reminding us in an ominous voice of the fact which roused our envy just as much as our dread, 'Billy Whittaker was in an iron lung two years ago. Infantile paralysis.'

Some people were lucky. None of us dared to hope that we would ever be surrounded by the glamour of an iron lung; we would have to be content all our lives with paltry flesh lungs.

'Well are we going to the Reservoir or not?'

That was someone trying to sound bossy like our father, – 'Well am I to have salmon sandwiches or not, am I to have lunch at all today or not?'

We struck our sticks in the air. They made a whistling sound. They were supple and young. We had tried to make musical instruments out of them, time after time we hacked at the willow and the elder to make pipes to blow our music, but no sound came but our own voices. And why did two sticks rubbed together not make fire? Why couldn't we ever *make* anything out of the bits of the world lying about us?

An airplane passed in the sky. We craned our necks to read the writing on the underwing, for we collected airplane numbers.

The plane was gone, in a glint of sun.

'Are we?' someone said.

'If there's an eclipse you can't see at all. The birds stop singing and go to bed.'

'Well are we?'

Certainly we were. We had not quelled all our misgiving, but we set out to follow the creek to the Reservoir.

What is it? I wondered. They said it was a lake. I thought it was a bundle of darkness and great wheels which peeled and sliced you like an apple and drew you toward them with demonic force, in the same way that you were drawn beneath the wheels of a train if you stood too near the edge of the platform. That was the terrible danger when the Limited came rushing in and you had to approach to kiss arriving aunts.

We walked on and on, past wild sweet peas, clumps of cutty grass, horse mushrooms, ragwort, gorse, cabbage trees; and then, at the end of the gully, we came to strange territory, fences we did not know, with the barbed wire tearing at our skin and at our skirts put on over our bathing suits because we felt cold though the sun stayed in the sky.

We passed huge trees that lived with their heads in the sky, with their great arms and joints creaking with age and the burden of being trees, and their mazed and linked roots rubbed bare of earth, like bones with the flesh cleaned from them. There were strange gates to be opened or climbed over, new directions to be argued and plotted, notices which said TRESPASSERS WILL BE PROSECUTED BY ORDER. And there was the remote immovable sun shedding without gentleness its influence of burning upon us and upon the town, looking down from its heavens and considering our infantile-paralysis epidemic, and the children tired of holidays and wanting to go back to school with the new stiff books with their crackling pages, the scrubbed ruler with the sun rising on one side amidst the twelfths, tenths, millimeters, the new pencils to be sharpened with the pencil shavings flying in long pickets and light-brown curls scalloped with red or blue; the brown school, the bare floors, the clump clump in the corridors on wet days!

We came to a strange paddock, a bull-paddock with its occupant planted deep in the long grass, near the gate, a Jersey bull polished like a wardrobe, burnished like copper, heavy beams creaking in the wave and flow of the grass.

'Has it got a ring through its nose? Is it a real bull or a steer?'

Its nose was ringed which meant that its savagery was tamed, or so we thought; it could be tethered and led; even so, it had once been savage and it kept its pride, unlike the steers who pranced and huddled together and ran like water through the paddocks, made no impression, quarried no massive shape against the sky.

The bull stood alone.

Had not Mr Bennet been gored by a bull, his own tame bull, and been rushed to Glenham Hospital for thirty-three stitches? Remembering Mr Bennet we crept cautiously 13 close to the paddock fence, ready to escape.

Someone said, 'Look, it's pawing the ground!'

A bull which pawed the ground was preparing for a charge. We escaped quickly through the fence. Then, plucking courage, we skirted the bushes on the far side of the paddock, climbed through the fence, and continued our walk to the Reservoir.

We had lost the creek between deep banks. We saw it now before us, and hailed it with more relief than we felt, for in its hidden course through the bull-paddock it had undergone change, it had adopted the shape, depth, mood of foreign water, foaming in a way we did not recognize as belonging to our special creek, giving no hint of its depth. It seemed to flow close to its concealed bed, not wishing any more to communicate with us. We realized with dismay that we had suddenly lost possession of our creek. Who had taken it? Why did it not belong to us any more? We hit our sticks in the air and forgot our dismay. We grew cheerful.

Till someone said that it was getting late, and we reminded one another that during the day the sun doesn't seem to move, it just remains pinned with a drawing pin against the sky, and then, while you are not looking, it suddenly slides down quick as the chopped-off head of a golden eel, into the sea, making everything in the world go dark.

'That's only in the tropics!'

We were not in the tropics. The divisions of the world in the atlas, the different colored cubicles of latitude and longitude fascinated us.

'The sand freezes in the desert at night. Ladies wear bits of sand. . . .'

'grains . . .'

'grains or bits of sand as necklaces, and the camels . . .'

'with necks like snails . . .'

'with horns, do they have horns?'

'Minnie Stocks goes with boys. . . .'

'I know who your boy is, I know who your boy is. . . .'

> Waiting by the garden gate,
> Waiting by the garden gate . . .

'We'll never get to the Reservoir!'

'Whose idea was it?'

'I've strained my ankle!'

Someone began to cry. We stopped walking.

'I've strained my ankle!'

There was an argument.

'It's not strained, it's sprained.'

'strained.'

'sprained.'

'All right sprained then. I'll have to wear a bandage, I'll have to walk on crutches. . . .'

'I had crutches once. Look. I've got a scar where I fell off my stilts. It's a white scar, like a centipede. It's on my shins.'

'Shins! Isn't it a funny word? Shins. Have you ever been kicked in the shins?'

'shins, funnybone . . .'

'it's humerus. . . .'

'knuckles . . .'

'a sprained ankle . . .'

'a strained ankle . . .'

'a whitlow, an ingrown toenail the roots of my hair warts spinal meningitis infantile paralysis . . .'

'Infantile paralysis, Infantile paralysis you have to be wheeled in a chair and wear irons on your legs and your knees knock together. . . .'

'Once you're in an iron lung you can't get out, they lock it, like a cage. . . .'

'You go in the amberlance . . .'

'*ambulance* . . .'

'amberlance . . .'

'ambulance to the hostible . . .'

'the *hospital*, an *amberlance to the hospital* . . .'

'Infantile Paralysis . . .'

'Friar's Balsam! Friar's Balsam!'

'Baxter's Lung Preserver, Baxter's Lung Preserver!'

'Syrup of Figs, California Syrup of Figs!'

'The creek's going on high-flow!'

Yes, there were bubbles on the surface, and the water was turning muddy. Our doubts were dispelled. It was the same old creek, and there, suddenly, just ahead, was a plantation of pine trees, and already the sighing sound of it reached our ears and troubled us. We approached it, staying close to the banks of our newly claimed creek, until once again the creek deserted us, flowing its own private course where we could not follow, and we found ourselves among the pine trees, a narrow strip of them, and beyond lay a vast surface of sparkling water, dazzling our eyes, its center chopped by tiny gray waves. Not a lake, nor a river, nor a sea.

'The Reservoir!'

The damp smell of the pine needles caught in our breath. There were no birds, only the constant sighing of the trees. We could see the water clearly now; it lay, except for the waves beyond the shore, in an almost perfect calm which we knew to be deceptive – else why were people so afraid of the Reservoir? The fringe of young pines on the edge, like toy trees, subjected to the wind, sighed and told us their sad secrets. In the Reservoir there was an appearance of neatness which concealed a disarray too frightening to be acknowledged except, without any defense, in moments of deep sleep and dreaming. The little sparkling innocent waves shone now green, now gray, petticoats, lettuce leaves; the trees sighed, and told us to be quiet, hush-sh, as if something were sleeping and should not be disturbed – perhaps that was what the trees were always telling us, to hush-sh in case we disturbed something which must never ever be awakened?

What was it? Was it sleeping in the Reservoir? Was that why people were afraid of the Reservoir?

Well we were not afraid of it, oh no, it was only the Reservoir, it was nothing to be afraid of, it was just a flat Reservoir with a fence around it, and trees, and on the far side a little house (with wheels inside?), and nothing to be afraid of.

'The Reservoir, The Reservoir!'

A noticeboard said DANGER, RESERVOIR.

Overcome with sudden glee we climbed through the fence and swung on the lower branches of the trees, shouting at intervals, gazing possessively and delightedly at the sheet of water with its wonderful calm and menace.

'The Reservoir! The Reservoir! The Reservoir!'

We quarreled again about how to pronounce and spell the word.

Then it seemed to be getting dark – or was it that the trees were stealing the sunlight and keeping it above their heads? One of us began to run. We all ran, suddenly, wildly, not caring about our strained or sprained ankles, through the trees out into the sun where the creek, but it was our creek no longer, waited for us. We wished it were our creek, how we wished it were our creek! We had lost all account of time. Was it nearly night? Would darkness overtake us, would we have to sleep on the banks of the creek that did not belong to us any more, among the wild sweet peas and the tussocks and the dead sheep? And would the eels come up out of the creek, as people said they did, and on their travels through the paddocks would they change into people who would threaten us and bar our way, TRESPASS-ERS WILL BE PROSECUTED, standing arm in arm in their black glossy coats, swaying, their mouths open, ready to swallow us? Would they ever let us go home, past the orchards, along the gully? Perhaps they would give us

Infantile Paralysis, perhaps we would never be able to walk home, and no one would know where we were, to bring us an iron lung with its own special key!

We arrived home, panting and scratched. How strange! The sun was still in the same place in the sky!

The question troubled us, 'Should we tell?'

The answer was decided for us. Our mother greeted us as we went in the door with, 'You haven't been long away, kiddies. Where have you been? I hope you didn't go anywhere near the Reservoir.'

Our father looked up from reading his newspapers.

'Don't let me catch you going near the Reservoir!'

We said nothing. How out-of-date they were! They were actually afraid!

Royal Icing

My mother had no money and no clothes except for an old sack tied around her waist, and a costume, with moth balls in the pockets, hanging in the front wardrobe. Her titties were flat and heavy against her tummy. Her legs had varicose veins. Her forehead was damp with steam or sweat or something which, sighing and waving her powerful arms in the humid air, she called 'atmosphere.'

'The atmosphere's very heavy today,' she would remark. 'It's something in the atmosphere that is responsible.'

Responsibility was a terrible substance to be apportioned, and mostly it came to rest upon the government; but the atmosphere could accept it just as well.

With so much, then, in the atmosphere, why did my mother want to bother with a set of icing-forcers?

She was a poor housekeeper, people said.

She was soft, they said.

We knew. We banged on the bedroom wall, 'Mum, bring us a piece!'

She brought us a piece of bread and jam.

We tore the wallpaper and poked our fingers through the

scrim, looking for secret documents. We ripped the inside from the cupboard, looking for secret panels. We broke the locks on the door, trying to be burglars. We climbed on the roof and bent the spouting. We kept dogs which fussed about us with wet noses, and my father scratched for fleas in the night, keeping a torch by the bed to save electricity, and leaping up and down at all hours crying, 'Got one, Got one, Hear them Crack?'

He lay the dead fleas in a row on the washstand, to compare each night's tally the following morning. It did not seem possible that so many fleas could have come to live in our house; they did not know evidently that our house was haunted in the shower in the bathroom where a former tenant had cut his throat with a razor. Or perhaps fleas were not concerned with such details.

And still, twice a year, Christmas and New Year, the cakes were baked and there was no icing-forcer to write professional greetings upon them or arrange the icing in patterns of leaves and petals.

'I tell you what,' my father said one day as he watched my mother icing the Christmas cake. 'We need a set of those things, you know they use them for icing cakes.'

'One of these days,' my mother said. 'We never know, do we, one of these days?'

'Who knows?' my father said.

That was a mysterious conversation. My father gave it up and settled down again to sew the straps on his workbag, for he believed in making his own workbag; while my mother continued icing the cake, dipping the knife in hot water and spreading, coaxing, trying not to mind when the stuff ran down the sides of the cake and the pink icing flowed into the white.

And so our lives continued and we did not think that fact mysterious because we expected it; aunts, uncles, grandparents, people over the road or in the next street were for dying in the end but we were for being alive; with so many fat spaniel dogs lying down in the corner of the washhouse to have puppies, we had no choice.

The fleas were such a worry. What if they spread to the neighbors? Not all my father's cleverness could get rid of them. And my father was very clever. He sewed and painted pictures on velvet cushion covers, he painted in oils, he dug beautiful double depths in the garden to plant the potatoes, he danced the Highland Fling and the Sword Dance and a dance where he sang

> *I'd rather have a hard-boiled egg,*
> *I'd rather have a hard-boiled egg;*

he could play the bagpipes and sing 'Ragtime Cowboy Joe.' But still he did not earn enough money to buy a set of icing-forcers in order to write greetings on the Christmas and New Year cakes.

'They're like guns,' my mother said dreamily. 'You can use them for shooting out biscuit dough into any shape you want.'

'You'll need to keep them clean,' my father warned her.

My mother was not expert at cleaning, she was not interested in sweeping four corners of a room and peering under the mat to surprise the dust-in-hiding. No. She stood at the back door and stared at the sunset over Weston, Waiareka, and Wainakarua, and sighed.

'Oh, oh,' I said to myself, 'what do you need to be happy?'

I longed for happiness and complete satisfaction.

Yet there wasn't a mincer in the house! How could anyone be happy without a mincer? Something had broken in our old mincer, and anyway the parts were lost and rusted and the main body of it was lying in a corner of the wash house beside the firewood, the old *Free Lance* magazines, and cast-out envelopes full of useless Tatts Results. I gave up hope of ever again having a mincer and being able to watch the mince coming out bright red with white flecks into the dish. I had given up longing for so many things which I desperately needed – long straight hair kept in place by a clasp or ribbon, a film test to get me to Hollywood where I would sing, amazing everyone, '*Oh the days are gone since beauty bright my heart's chain wore,*' and,

> *I had a pal Blackie so dear to my heart,*
> *but the warders they shot him . . .*'

an everlasting ticket to the pictures, dancing lessons, the bills all paid, a different mother in a white dress, a father who did not keep saying, in spite of his cleverness, 'You'll feel the back of my hand in a moment,' 'I'll warm your bottom if I get hold of you. . . .' So many needs.

It was true that we had a separator which whined and trembled and vibrated, and I would stand on a chair and pour the foamy new milk into the bowl at the top. The bowl was a most beautiful shape, containing, generous, and even if the cows were in full milk the bowl never overflowed. I used to watch the skim milk pouring, spurting from the silver-colored tube, and the cream dripping in fat blobs into the jug on the other side.

'Skim milk!' my mother said in horror. 'Never drink skim milk!'

I used to pat the butter together with the scrubbed ribbed butter pats.

So. A separator, an old mincer – were they enough to guarantee happiness?

Also, I had a possie of my own under the silver birch trees. I had a pet cockabully which I had tamed myself, and which came when I called it, although it had no choice because it lived in a restricted area and just happened to be near.

But these were not enough. It seemed that nothing was ever enough.

Year after year my mother said, 'We need a set of those things that bakers use to ice their cakes.'

And year after year my father agreed.

'It would be nice, dandy in fact,' he said. 'We do need a new mincer as well, you know.'

For a short time of suspense there was declared competition between the superiority of a mincer and a set of icing-forcers; neither won. Whenever my father wanted Shepherd's Pie for dinner the meat was chopped by hand, and when Christmas and New Year came the cakes were iced without the adroit targeting of an icing-forcer.

We grew up. We left school and home and sent sudden telegrams during the week, ARRIVING MIDNIGHT TRAIN. There was something at home which we expected to find during the weekend, something which had haunted us while we were absent, enticed us with images of peace and comfort; yet, strangely, when we had left our cup of hot cocoa and gone tiptoe to our room with its musty smell and its shelves of already worm-attended books, we knew a feeling of disillusionment, of having been cheated. The something was as out of our reach as the new mincer, the set of icing-forcers.

My father retired, with a dinner set as a present.

My mother's hair went white, suddenly, as if she had been shocked in the night by a presence which was revealed to her alone; no one knew its identity; she was acquainted with more things in the atmosphere than we dreamed of.

Then one day my father arrived home with a parcel which he opened on the kitchen table.

'See,' he said, and spilled the metal parts from their cardboard box onto the oilcloth. 'See, you can use it for writing on cakes, for arranging the dough of biscuits, remember how we've always wanted it?'

My mother gazed in admiration. 'So many parts!' she exclaimed, and proceeded to count them. 'Why, there must be about ten! And all different! Of course I don't make cakes every day, and now that the children aren't home . . .'

'But at Christmas, and New Year, and for visitors. Just look,' my father said, taking each part separately and holding it up to the light, like a bank clerk testing money to decide if it were counterfeit or genuine. He twirled the parts, gently, protectively, like coins, upon the table, listening carefully. 'Look. Perfect.'

Then his face became serious and stern. 'They'll have to be cleaned thoroughly after use,' he said. 'And dried on the rack above the fire. We don't want them getting rusty, like the mincer, or stuck with scum, like the separator.'

'No of course not,' my mother said, looking guilty and afraid.

After all, a set of icing-forcers was a grave responsibility, and now that she was growing older she was finding it more difficult to perform the agility known as 'coping' which I had long fancied to mean creeping up to one's enemies, unsuspected, and enveloping them in a dark cloth, perhaps smothering them.

My mother had a natural difficulty in coping.

With the icing set there seemed to be so many parts, so many complicated instructions printed in the leaflet, and all merely to write Merry Christmas, Happy New Year upon two cakes to make them appear as if they had been baked at the baker's!

Christmas came. The cake was baked, and when it had cooled my mother iced it the old way, dipping a knife in hot water, and plowing the icing like a field of snow across the top of the cake.

'You never used the icing set,' my father accused.

My mother flushed guiltily. 'Well,' she said, hesitating.

'You might have used them,' my father persisted. 'It's only twice a year.'

She was thoughtful a moment.

'Couldn't we exchange them?'

My father looked horrified. 'After all these years! Isn't it what we've always wanted? No. It's true what you say, Mum, they're not really much use.'

But they did not exchange them. Both my mother and my father appreciated the set. Sometimes when it was my father's habit to bring out the Postcards he had brought back from the War, his book of fishing flies, or back numbers of the *Railway Magazine*, he would fetch the icing set as well, taking it from its cardboard box and spilling the parts upon the table where he would carefully handle each one, as if he were a collector perusing valuable stamps or coins.

My mother gave the icing set a special place on the sideboard beside the few pieces of china which were too good to be used and the pair of little blue glass slippers which had been sent with Auntie Maggie's things when she died, and which now housed buttons, domes, needles, hooks and eyes. But the icing set was never used. It became a landmark on the sideboard.

'It's behind the icing set.'

'It's to the left of the icing set.'

'It's just in front of the icing set.'

And my mother and father were growing old without ever writing festive messages upon the Christmas and New Year cakes!

My mother was afraid of Death. She saw Death sometimes. He would be bending over the coal in the coal house, or in the garden tying up the broad beans or the sweet peas that had strayed from their trellis. Sometimes he sat in the sun with his hands in his lap, snoring. He could afford to snore. And still the icing set stayed on the sideboard next to the best china and the little blue glass slippers, and between my mother and my father on one side, and Death on the other there was a diminishing gulf to be filled or concealed in some way; the years of their lives were like a slowly closing wound where the edges must be prevented at all costs from uniting.

What dreams were left for them now to wedge between birth and death?

Perhaps to stretch life, like a tightening shoe, to make it fit for ever and ever?

Tell me, what do we need? What dream must we pursue and not be afraid to grasp and possess when it finally becomes reality? Is it better to want and get an icing-forcer, a mincer, than to walk for the remainder of our lives about the house with a little dagger in our pocket trying to catch

Death bending over the coal in the coal house or tying up the stray broad beans or sweet peas on the trellis, or sitting in the sun snoring? Trying to catch and kill him, and then, with a surprised look on our face, turning the dagger to our own heart?

The Teacup

When he came to live in the same house she hoped that he would be friendlier, take a deeper interest in her, invite her to the pictures or to go dancing with him or in the summer walking arm in arm in the park. They might even go for a day to the seaside, she thought, or on one of those bus tours visiting Windsor Castle, London Airport, or the Kentish Hopfields. How exciting it would be!

He had been working at the factory for over two years now, since he came out of the Army, and they had often spoken to each other during the day, shared football coupons and bets in the Grand National, lunched together at the staff canteen where you could get a decent meal for two and ten, extra for tea, coffee, and bread and butter. He had talked to her of his family, how they were all dead except his brother and himself; of his life in the Army, traveling the world, a good life, India, Japan, Germany. Once or twice he had mentioned (this was certain and had made her heart flurry) that he would like to 'find someone and settle down.'

He needs someone, she thought. He is quite alone and needs someone.

She told him of her own life, how she had thought of emigrating to Australia and had gone to Australia House where an official asked her age and when she told him he said sharply, 'We are looking for younger people; the young and the skilled.'

She was forty-four. They did not want people of forty-four in Australia. Not single women.

'They wouldn't take me either,' he had said, and, quick with sympathy she had exclaimed, 'Oh, Bill!'

She had never called him by his first name before. He had always been Mr Forest. He addressed her as Miss Rogers, but she knew that if they became closer friends he would call her Edith, that is, Edie. She told him that she was staying in South London, living in a room in a house belonging to this family; that she knitted jerseys for the little girl, helped the landlady with the washing and sewing, and looked after the bird and the cat when the family went on holiday. She told how regularly every second weekend she stayed with her sister at Blackheath, for a change; how her other sister had emigrated years ago to Australia and now was married with three children and a house of her own, she sent photos of the family, you could see them outside in the garden in the sun and how brown the children looked and the garden was bright with flowers, tropical blooms that you never see in England except in Kew Gardens, and wasn't it hot there under glass among the rubber plants? But the photos never showed her sister's husband, for they were separated, he had left her; her other sister's husband had gone too, packed up and vanished, even while his daughter still suffered from back trouble and now she was grown up and crippled, lying on the sofa all day, but managing wonderfully with the district nurse coming on Wednesday afternoons, no, Tuesdays, Wednesday was early closing. And her sister's son had a grant to study accountancy, he would qualify, there was a future ahead of him. . . .

So they talked together, and soon it was commonplace for him to call her Edith (not Edie, not yet) and her to say Bill, though in front of the others at work they still said Miss Rogers and Mr Forest. Then one night she invited him home for tea, and he accepted the invitation. How happy she was that evening! How she wished it had been her own home with her own furniture and curtains and not just one room and the small shared kitchen but two or three or four rooms to walk in and out of, opening and closing the doors, each room serving its purpose, one for visitors, another . . .

She bought extra food that evening, far too much, and it turned out that he didn't care for what she had bought, and he didn't mind saying so, politely of course, but he had been in the Army and was used to speaking his mind.

'There's no fuss in the Army. You say what you think.'

'Of course it's best,' she said, trying not to sound disappointed because he did not care for golden sponge pudding and had preferred not to sample the peeled shrimps, cocktail brand.

But on the whole they spent a pleasant evening. She

knitted, and showed him photographs of her family. They went for a short walk in the park and while they were walking she linked her arm with his, as she had seen other women do, and her eyes were bright with happiness. She mentioned to him that a small room was vacant on the top floor where she stayed, and that if ever he decided to change his lodging wouldn't it be a good idea if he took the room?

She could manage things for him; she could arrange meals, see to shopping and washing; he would be independent of course. . . .

A few weeks later when he had been on holiday at his brother's and had arrived back at his lodgings only to find that the two women of the house, having decided after waiting long enough that he was definitely not going to ask one of them to marry him, had given him notice to leave, he remembered the vacancy that Miss Rogers – Edith – had mentioned, and one week later he had come to live in the house, half a flight of stairs up from her own room.

She helped to prepare his room. She cleaned the windows and drew the curtains wide to give him full advantage of the view – the back gardens of the two or three adjacent houses, the road beyond, with the Pink Paraffin lorries parked outside their store; the garden of the large house belonging to the County Councilor.

She made the bed, draping the candlewick bedspread, shelving it at the top beneath the pillows, shifting the small table from the corner near the door to a more convenient position near the head of the bed.

A reading lamp? Would he need a reading lamp?

With a tremble of excitement she realized that she knew nothing about him, that from now on, each day would be filled to the brim with discovery. Either he read in bed or he didn't read in bed. Did he like a cup of tea in the early morning? What did he do in the evenings? What did he sound like when he coughed in the middle of the night when all was quiet?

Downstairs in the small kitchen which she shared with Jean, another lodger in the house, an unmarried woman a few years younger than herself, she segregated on a special shelf covered by half a yard of green plastic which hung, scalloped at the edge, the utensils he would need for his meals; his own special spoon, knife, fork. On the top shelf there were two large cups, one with the handle broken. Jean had broken it. She had confessed long ago but the subject still came up between her and Edith and always served to discharge irritation between them.

As Edith was choosing the special teacup to be used solely by Bill, she picked up the handleless one, and remarked to Jean, 'These are nice cups, they hold plenty of tea, but that woman from Australia who used to stay in the room before you came, she broke the handle off this cup.'

'No, I broke it,' Jean confessed again.

'No. It was that woman from Australia who stayed here in the room before you came. I was going to emigrate to Australia once. I went as far as getting the papers and filling them in.'

The woman from Australia had also been responsible for other breakages and inconveniences. She had never cleaned the gas stove, she had blocked the sink with vegetables, she hadn't fitted in with arrangements for bathing and washing, and the steam from her baths had peeled the wallpaper off the bathroom wall, newly decorated too. She had left behind a miscellany of objects which were labeled as 'belonging to the woman from Australia' and which Edith carefully preserved and replaced when the cupboards were cleaned out, as if the woman from Australia were still a needful presence in the house.

Attached to the special shelf prepared for Bill there was a row of golden cuphooks; upon one of them Edith hung the teacup she had chosen for him, a large deep cup with a gold, green and dark-blue pattern around the rim and the words ARKLOW POTTERY EIRE DONEGAL, encircled by a smudged blue capital *E*, printed underneath. In every way the teacup seemed specially right for Bill. How Edith longed for him to be settled in, having his tea, with her pouring from the new teapot warmed under its new cozy, into his special teacup!

He took two heaped spoons of sugar, she shivered with excitement at remembering.

On Bill's first night she could not disguise her happiness. They left work together that night, they came home sitting side by side on the top deck of the bus, they walked together from the bus stop down and along the road to the house. His luggage had already been delivered; it stood in the corridor, strapped and bulging, mysterious, exciting, with foreign labels.

And now there was the bliss of showing him his room, the ins and outs of his new lodgings – the bathroom, telling him on which day he could bathe, showing him how to turn on the hot water.

'Up is on, Down is off. . . .'

Explaining, pointing out, revealing, with her cheeks flushed and her breast rising and falling quickly to get enough breath for speech because the details, all the pointing out and revealing were fraught with so much excitement.

At last she led him to the cupboard in the kitchen.

'This is your shelf. Here is your knife, fork, spoon. Of course you can always take anything, anything you want from my shelf, here, this one here, but not from Jean's.'

'Anything you want,' she said again, urgently, 'take from my shelf, won't you?'

Then she paused.

'And this is your special cup and saucer.'

She detached the cup from its golden hook and held it to the light. He looked approvingly at it.

'Nice and big,' he said.

She glowed.

'That's why I chose it from the others. There used to be two of them, but that woman from Australia who stayed here broke the handle of one.'

She still held the teacup as if she were reluctant to return
36   it to its place on the hook.

'Isn't it roomy?' she said, seeking, in a way, for further acknowledgement from him.

But he had turned his attention elsewhere. He was hungry. He sniffed at the food already cooking.

They had dinner then. She had prepared everything – the stewed beef, potatoes, carrots, onions, cabbage. His place was laid at the small table which was really a cabinet and was therefore awkward to sit at, as one's knees bumped into its cupboard door. She apologized for the table, and thought, I'll have to look around for a cheap table, perhaps one with a formica top, easily cleaned, Oh dear there is so much furniture we need, and those lace curtains need renewing, just from where I am sitting I can see they are almost in shreds.

And she sighed with the happy responsibility of everything.

After dinner she washed the dishes, showed him where to hang his bath towel, and where to put his shaving gear, before he went upstairs to lie on his bed and read the evening paper. Then, sharp at half-past eight, she put the kettle on (she hadn't noticed before how furred it was, and dented at the sides, she would have to see about a new kettle) and when the water was boiling she made two cups of tea, taking one up to his room and knocking gently on the door.

'Can I come in, Bill?'

'Yes, come in.'

He was rather irritated at being interrupted, and showed 37

his irritation by frowning at her, for he had of course been in the Army and he believed in directness, in speaking out.

She stood a moment, timidly, in the doorway.

'I've brought you a cup of tea.'

She handed him his special teacup on its matching saucer.

'That's good of you.'

He took it, and blew the parcels from the top. She stayed a while, talking, while he drank his tea. She asked him how he liked his new lodging. She told him there were a few shops around the corner, two cinemas further down the road 'showing nice programs of an evening,' and that in summer the park nearby was lovely to sit and walk in.

Then he told her that he was tired, all this changing around, that he was going to bed to get some sleep.

'See you in the morning,' she said.

She took the cups and went downstairs to the kitchen to tidy up for the night. Jean was in the kitchen filling her hot-water bottle. Edith glanced at her, not being able to conceal her joy. Jean had no friend to stay, she had no one to cook for, to wash for. Edith began to talk of Bill.

'I'll be up earlier than usual tomorrow,' she said. 'There's Bill's breakfast to get. He has two boiled eggs every morning,' she said, pausing for Jean to express the wonder which should be aroused at the thought of two boiled eggs for breakfast.

'Does he?' Jean exclaimed, faintly admiring, envious.

'I'm calling him in the morning as he finds it difficult to
38 wake up. Some men do, you know.'

'Yes,' Jean said. 'I know.'

Early next morning Edith was bustling about the kitchen attending to Bill and his toilet and breakfast needs – putting on hot water for the shave, boiling the two eggs, and then sharp at twenty to eight they set out together to catch the bus for work, walking up the road arm in arm. Bill wore a navy-blue duffle coat and carried a canvas bag. The morning light caught the sandy color of his thinning hair, and showed the pink baldness near his temples and the pink confectionery tint of his cheeks. She was wearing her heavy brown tweed coat and the fawn flowerpot hat which she had bought when her sister took her shopping at Blackheath. Clothes were cheaper yet more attractive in Blackheath; the market was full of bargains – why was it not so, Edith wondered, in her home territory, why did other people always live where really good things were marked down, going for a song, though the flowerpot hat was not cheap. Edith had long ago given up worrying over the hat. She had felt uneasy about it – perhaps it would go suddenly out of fashion, and although she never kept consciously in fashion, whenever there was a topsy-turvy revolution with waists going up or down and busts being annihilated, Edith had the feeling that the rest of the world had turned a corner and abandoned her. She felt confused, not knowing which track to follow; people were pressing urgently forward, their destinations known and planned, young girls too, half her age. . . .

Edith felt bitter toward the young girls. Why, the tips of 39 their shoes were like hooks or swords, anyone could see they were a danger.

But everything was different now: there was Bill.

Each night they walked home, again arm in arm, separating at the shops where Edith bought supplies for their dinner while Bill went on to the house, put his bag away, had a wash, and sat cozily on a chair in the kitchen, reading the evening paper and waiting for his dinner to be prepared. They had dinner, sitting awkwardly at the table-cabinet, with Edith each night apologizing, remarking that one weekend she would scout around at Blackheath for a cheap table.

'The wallpaper wants doing too,' she said one evening, looking thoughtfully at the torn paper over the fireplace. To her joy Bill took the hint.

'I'm not bad at decorating,' he said. 'Being in the Army, you know.'

She laughed impatiently and blushed.

'But you're not in the Army now, you're settling down!'

He agreed. 'Yes, it's time I settled down.'

He spent the following weekend preparing the kitchen, and although it was Edith's usual time for visiting her sister, she did not go to Blackheath but stayed in the kitchen, making cups of tea for Bill, fetching, carrying, admiring, talking to him, holding equipment for him, and by Sunday evening when the job was finished and the kitchen cupboard had been painted too, and the window sills, and even new curtains hung on plastic hooks which were rustproof and could be washed free of dust and soot, the two sat together, in deep contentment, drinking their cups of tea and eating their slices of white bread and apricot jam, homemade.

But Edith's satisfaction was chilled by the persistent thought, It isn't even my own home, it isn't even my own home. Still, she consoled herself, in time, who knows?

Their routine was established. Every evening it was the same – dinner, apologies over the awkward shape of the table (but why, she thought, should I spend money on a table when it isn't even my own home?), meager conversation, a few exclamations, statements, revival of rumors; the newspapers to read. . . . They each bought their own evening paper, and after they both had finished reading they exchanged papers, with a dreamlike movement, for they were at the same time concentrating on their stewed beef or fried chops or fish.

'There's the same news in both, really.'

'Yes, there's not much difference.'

Nevertheless they exchanged papers and settled once more to eat and read. When they had finished she would say, 'I'll do the dishes.'

At first Bill used to walk around with a tea towel hanging over his arm. Later, when he realized that his help was not needed, he didn't bother to remove the towel from the railing behind the kitchen door. There were three railings, one each for Edith, Jean, and Bill. Edith had bought Bill a 41 special tea towel, red and blue (colorfast) with a matador and two bulls printed on it.

One evening when Edith was not feeling tired she said she would like to go to the pictures, that there was a good one showing down the road, and if they hurried they would get in at the beginning of the main picture, or halfway through *Look at Life*.

Bill was not interested.

'Not for me, not tonight.'

He went upstairs to make the final preparations and judgments for the filling-in of the football coupon, while Edith retired to her room, switched on the electric fire, and sat in her armchair, knitting. The glow from the fire sent bars of light, like burns, across her face. Her eyes watered a little as she leaned forward to follow the pattern. The wool felt thick and rough against her fingers.

I must be tired after all, she thought, and put down her knitting.

At half-past eight she went to the kitchen to make the usual cup of tea, and as she said good night to Bill she thought, He's tired after that heavy packing at work all day. Maybe in the weekends we'll go out together somewhere, to the pictures or the park.

The next morning when it was time to set out for work it seemed that Bill was not quite ready, there were a few things to see to, he said. So Edith went alone up the road to the bus stop, and later Bill set out for work alone. And that night they came home separately. And after that, every morning and evening they went to and from work alone.

In the weekend Bill mentioned that he knew friends who kept a pub in Covent Garden, that he would be spending the weekend there. Soon he spent every weekend there. At night he still came home for meals, but sometimes he neglected to say that he wasn't coming home, and Edith would make elaborate preparations for dinner, only to find that she had to eat it alone.

'If only he would tell me,' she complained to Jean. 'I see him at work during the day, and for some reason he's even ashamed to let on that he stays here. Afraid the others will tease him.'

She smiled wistfully, a little secretively, as if perhaps there might be cause for teasing.

Well, she thought, at least he sleeps here.

And was there not all the satisfying flurry in the morning of heating his shaving-water, putting the two eggs to boil, leaving the kettle on low gas in case he needed it, setting his place at the table with his plate, his knife, and, carefully at the side, his special teacup and saucer? And then taking possession of details concerning him, as if they were property being signed to her alone? He eats far too much salt. One drum of salt lasts no time with him. How can he eat so much black pudding? He's fond of sugar, too.

He likes, he prefers, he would rather have . . .

He'd be lost without his cup of tea.

Yes, that was one thing he was always ready for, she could always make him a cup of tea.

And then there were his personal habits which she treasured as legacies, as if his gradual withdrawal from her had been concerned, in a way, with death, wills and next-of-kin, with her being the sole beneficiary.

'Why, oh why, does he leave all his pairs of socks to be washed at once?' – said in a voice at the same time complaining and proud – 'I've told him to bring his dirty clothing down for me to wash, but he persists in leaving it in his room, and there I have to go and search about in his most private clothing, and I never know where he keeps anything!' – said in a voice warm with satisfaction.

It was true that her washing seemed endless, and lasted all Saturday morning, and the ironing took all Sunday morning or Monday evening. She liked ironing his shirts, underclothes and handkerchiefs. She tried to accept the fact that he was not inclined to take her out anywhere, not even to the pictures or the park, that he did not care to accompany her to or from work. Once or twice she reminded him that he was getting old, that he was forty-seven, that she was about the same age . . . perhaps they could spend the rest of their lives together, life was not all dizzy romance, perhaps they could marry . . . she would look after him, see to him. . . .

'But I like my freedom,' he said.

Then she tried to frighten him into thoughts of himself as a lonely old man with no one to care for him and no one to talk to.

'If it happens,' he said 'it happens. I've been in the Army, you know, around in Japan, India, Germany, I've seen a thing or two.'

As if being in the Army had provided him with special defenses and privileges. And it had, hadn't it? He could speak his mind, he knew what he was up to. . . .

So the wonderful hopes which had filled Edith's mind when Bill had first come to stay, began to fade. Why won't he see? she thought. I'm trying to do my best for him. It would be nice, in summer, to walk arm in arm in the park.

Meanwhile her stated attitude became, I don't care, it doesn't worry me.

The Council were starting a course of dancing lessons for beginners over thirty. She began to go dancing in the evenings, and when she came home she would tell Jean about the lovely time she had enjoyed.

'I go with the girl from work. Her father has that gray Jaguar with the toy leopard in the back.'

'You want to go dancing,' she suggested one night to Jean.

'Oh,' Jean replied. 'I had a friend to visit me.'

'A friend? A man?'

'Yes. A man.'

'I didn't see him.'

'Oh, he came to visit me.'

Sometimes Edith went dancing twice a week now, and Bill came home or didn't come home to dinner. Still, rather wistfully, Edith prepared food for him, peeled the potatoes (he was fond of potatoes), cleaned the Brussels sprouts, or 45 left little notes with directions in them: 'The sausages from yesterday are in the oven if you care for them. There's soup in the enamel jug. There are half a dozen best eggs on my shelf . . . or if you fancy baked beans . . .'

Edith noticed that Jean's new friend seemed to bring her a plentiful supply of food. Why, sometimes her shelf was filled to overflowing. She hoped that Bill had remembered not to touch anything upon Jean's shelf.

'My friend's good that way,' Jean said. 'And he always lets me know when he is coming to visit me.'

Edith flushed.

'Bill would let me know about dinner and suchlike, but I don't see him much during the day, not now he's working upstairs. He's very thoughtful underneath, Bill is.'

'My friend bought me underwear for Christmas. Do you think I should have accepted it?'

'It's rather personal isn't it?'

Bill had not given Edith a present.

'Oh there's nothing between us,' Jean assured her.

'Bill wanted to give me something but I wouldn't have it. I said I enjoy what I'm doing for him and that's that. You say your friend came on Saturday? I've never seen him yet.'

'You always miss him, don't you?'

That was Monday.

That night when Bill had come home, eaten his dinner, and gone to his room, and Edith had put the kettle on the gas and was setting out the cups for tea, she noticed that

Bill's cup was missing, the big teacup with the gold, dark-blue and light-green decorations and the words printed at the bottom, the big teacup, Bill's cup, that hung always on the golden hook.

With a feeling of panic she searched Bill's shelf, Jean's, her own, and the cupboards underneath, removing the grater and flour sifter, the cake tins, and the two battered saucepans which had belonged to the woman from Australia.

She could not find the teacup.

She hurried from the kitchen and up to Bill's room.

'Bill,' she called, 'your cup's missing!'

A sleepy voice sounded, 'My what?'

She opened the door. He was lying fully dressed on the bed.

He sat up.

Edith's voice was trembling, as if she were bringing him bad news which did not affect him as much as it affected herself, yet which she needed to share.

'Your big teacup that hangs on the hook on your shelf. Have you seen it?'

He spoke abruptly. 'No, I haven't seen it.'

She looked at him with all the feelings of the past weeks and months working in her face, and her eyes bright. Her voice implored him, 'Now Bill, just stay there quietly and try to remember when you last saw your cup!'

He got up from the bed. 'What the hell?' he shouted. 'What the hell is the fuss about?'

He lowered his voice. 'Well I last saw it on the ledge by

the cupboard. I had a cup of tea in it,' he said guiltily.

Then he saw the marks where his shoes had touched the end of the bed. He brushed at the counterpane. 'I should have taken my shoes off, eh?'

Edith was calm now. 'So you haven't seen your teacup?' she said, but she could not bear to dismiss the subject, to make an end of it all, without saying, 'Your teacup, Bill, the one with the gold, dark-blue and green that hangs on the hook on your shelf?'

Then she suddenly left him, and hurried down the stairs, and knocked sharply on Jean's door, and almost before she was invited, she opened the door and looked searchingly around the room. Her face was flushed. Her eyes were glistening as if she had been leaning too close to the fire. At first she did not speak but glanced meaningly at one of the kitchen cups which Jean had borrowed for a drink of water.

'Have you seen Bill's cup?' Edith asked, staring hard at the cup of water as if to say, 'If you borrow this you might surely have borrowed Bill's cup!'

Jean felt a pang of guilt. She had not seen or borrowed the cup but she felt sure that suspicion rested on her.

'No,' she said. 'I haven't seen it. Isn't it in the kitchen?'

'No, it's not there.'

Edith's voice had a note of desperation, as if the incident had brought her suddenly to the limit of her endurance.

'No, it's not there,' she said. She felt like weeping, but she was not going to break down, she had her suspicions of Jean. She looked once more around Jean's room, as if trying to uncover the hiding-place.

'I last saw it,' she said, 'on Saturday at lunchtime when I washed it. Then I went away to my sister's at Blackheath, as you know, and Bill went away for the weekend, and the family was away. That means you were the only one in the house.'

'My friend came,' Jean reminded her.

Edith pounced. 'Perhaps he used Bill's cup?'

No, Jean told her, he hadn't.

'Well you were the only one in the house from Saturday at lunchtime.'

'Perhaps Bill knows where it is?' Jean asked.

Edith's voice quavered. 'He doesn't. I've asked him. I said to him, "Now just sit quietly and remember when you last saw it."'

'What did he say?'

'He said when he last saw it, there were dregs of tea in it, and it was on the ledge by the cupboard in the kitchen. And that's correct,' Edith said triumphantly, 'for I washed it – ·you were the only one in the house with it until Monday, today, and between Saturday and today it vanished. There was your friend of course,' she said accusingly.

'Oh, he didn't touch it. I don't know what to do with him, he brings me so much food. And he always writes to tell me when he is visiting me.'

'Bill is a typical man,' Edith said coldly. 'He has no idea what food we (he and I) need. If he did he would buy it, and see to things. And now that he's upstairs at work during the day he can't see me to say whether or not he's coming home to dinner.'

Then she made a stifled sound, like a sob. 'I don't know where his cup has got to, his teacup.'

It seemed that the teacup hanging on its golden hook had contained the last of Edith's hope, and now it was gone, someone had taken it. She suspected Jean. Who was this mysterious friend who came to visit Jean? Jean hadn't discovered this friend until Bill had come to stay in the house. It was all Jean's fault, everything was Jean's fault, Jean was jealous of her and Bill, she had stolen Bill's teacup, his special teacup with the gold, dark-blue and green decorations, and the writing underneath. . . .

For the next few days there was tension between the two women.

Edith left a note before she went to work, 'Dear Jean, If you are ironing please will you run over Bill's two towels?'

Jean forgot to iron the towels.

Each evening the same questions and answers passed between them.

'Bill's cup must be somewhere. It just can't vanish. You didn't break it by chance, and put it in the rubbish tin?'

'If I had broken it I would have said.'

'That woman from Australia broke the handle of the other one, if that woman from Australia hadn't broken the other one Bill could be using it now.'

'*I* broke the other one.'

'Then you could have broken this one as well. But I

thought . . . that handle . . . I thought it was the woman from Australia. I tried to emigrate to Australia once. I went as far as getting papers and filling them in. . . .'

She spoke longingly as if emigrating to Australia were another of the good things in life which had been denied her at the last moment, as if it were somehow concerned with the affair of Bill and the lost teacup and never ever walking arm in arm in the park, in summer.

By the fourth day the kitchen had been thoroughly searched and the cup was nowhere to be found. Bill was now spending many of his week-nights away from the house, and the two women found themselves often alone together. They spoke little. They glanced grimly at each other, accusingly.

Sometimes at night in her room in the middle of reading her romantic novel from the library (*Set Fair for France, All My Own, Love and Ailsa Dare*), Edith would break down and weep, she could not explain it, but the disappearance of the teacup was the last straw. She said the phrase to herself, drying her eyes, 'The last straw.'

Then she chided herself, 'Don't be silly. What's the use?' But the people in the novels had everything so neatly provided for them. There was this secretary with the purple eyes and trim figure, and she dined by candlelight with the young director, the youngest and wealthiest director of the firm; everybody was jealous of this secretary; all the men made excuses to visit her at her desk, to invite her out. . . .

Edith was heavily built; she bought a salmon-pink corset

once a year; she needed to wear it. Her eyes were gray and chipped, like a pavement. Her back humped.

'I'm ugly of course,' she said, as she closed *Love and Ailsa Dare*. 'I don't mind that so much now I'm used to it, but the teacup, Bill's cup, who has taken it?'

After the week had passed and the cup had still not been found, and there was no clue to its hiding-place, Edith gave up preparing meals for Bill. She even neglected to go to his room to collect what he referred to as his 'mid-week smalls.' And the following week, in an effort to cheer herself, she went dancing three times to the Council class, but she found little pleasure in it. She had tried to buy a pair of white satin shoes such as everyone else wore, and when she did find a pair they nipped and crammed her two toes, causing a pain which was so prolonged that she visited the doctor (the one around the corner with his house newly decorated, and his smart car standing outside the gate; everyone went to him) who said to her, 'I can do nothing about it, it's your age, Miss Rogers, the best thing is for you to have a small operation which will remove those two toes; it's arthritis, it attacks the toes first, with some patients; the operation is quite quick and harmless.'

When Edith came home from the doctor's she burst into tears. Two toes removed, just like that! It was the beginning of the end. They would soon want permission to remove every part of her, they did that sort of thing, gradually, once they began they never knew where to finish.

She stopped going to dancing class. She stayed inside by

the electric fire, knitting, and sewing at the sewing machine, pedaling fiercely until her legs ached and she was forced to rest them.

One weekend when she returned from her sister's at Blackheath she found that Bill had changed his lodging, had gone to stay with his friends who kept the pub in Covent Garden. He had gone without telling her, without a word. But he never told people things, he was secretive, he didn't understand, he had been in the Army. . . .

That Monday evening on her way past the shops Edith saw Jean in the grocer's; she was buying food, mountains of it. So much for her mysterious friend, Edith thought, as she hurried home.

The two met later in the kitchen, filling their hot-water bottles.

'Have you been dancing lately?' Jean asked.

'Yes,' Edith said. 'I go often. In fact I went during the weekend. I had a wonderful time. Smashing. Did your friend come?'

'Yes, my friend came, with stacks of food, look!'

Jean pointed to the bread, fruit salad, ham, which she had just bought at the grocer's.

Then, without speaking much – for what was there to say? – they filled their hot-water bottles and said good night.

And no one ever found the dark-blue, gold, green teacup with the writing ARKLOW POTTERY EIRE DONEGAL underneath, that used to hang – an age ago, it seemed – in the kitchen on the special shelf on the shining golden hook!

A Night of Frost and a
Morning of Mist

After a night of frost and a morning of mist the day is cloudless. The men of the street have gone to work; the women remain, putting out the milk bottles, shaking the door mats, polishing the windows, dusting the window sills.

Early this morning when the sun had begun to shine warm against my window, a blowfly appeared, the first blowfly of spring, swaggering about in his new navy-blue suit, bumping upon the pane, knocking, clamoring. He skated, he buzzed, he walked upside down and sideways with his feet padded with death. He saw me watching him. He saw me reaching for yesterday's newspaper to fold and creep up and swipe him with it, for he knew that I hated him for appearing so boldly on a day which had emerged in such perfection from a night of frost and a morning of mist. He was a tiny but swelling speck that would block the sun and plunge the earth into darkness. I knew. I wielded my newspaper.

'Don't kill me,' he said, in that small voice used by insects, animals, furniture, who appear in fairy stories and startle people (the woodcutter, his son, the young man lying on the grassy bank in the wood, the servant girl sweeping the bedrooms of the palace) with their cries, 'Don't kill me, Help! Help!' He knew, however, that he lived in a modern age when cries for help are ignored when they are made by creatures whose feet are padded with death. So he decided to impress me with his fame.

'Do you know,' he said, 'that in the Science Museum there is an entire display devoted to my life cycle, with illustrations, models, comprehensive labels? Often my family and I put on our Sunday best and visit the Museum, and may I say that we are received with pleasure?'

The thought of his fame did not deter me from advancing with my folded newspaper. Again he cried, 'Help! Help!' Did anyone hear him, anyone engaged in present-day folklore – the builder on the new housing estate, the old man lying in the park in the sun, the junior sweeping the floor of the Beauty Parlor, the man from the Water Board inspecting the manhole covers in the street, the workmen replacing the broken paving stones, the woman with her canvas bag slung over her shoulders going from door to door distributing Free Offers, coupons for soap, frozen peas and spaghetti – those who traditionally receive the confidence of insects, animals, furniture, growing plants? Did they hear? Were they listening? Do they listen as carefully as the woodcutter used to do, and the servant girl sweeping the bedrooms of the palace?

'Don't kill me, help help!'

I struck the newspaper against the windowpane and the bossy blowfly was dead.

Then I looked out at the almost deserted street, at the early-spring sun shining down on the pavement stones, at the babies lying in their prams outside the houses, at the men digging up the road near the corner, surrounding themselves with bold notices, red flags, lanterns gleaming like rubies. Then outside my own room I glimpsed the tyrant of Grove Hill Road, a heavy-jowled black-and-white tomcat, the father of most of the kittens in Grove Hill Road, who carries in his head maps of dustbins, strategic positions of milk bottles, exact judgments of the height of garden and street wall, gate, and the wired street trees that now have tiny pink buds on them, like dolly mixture. The tom has long black whiskers. He was sitting on the gatepost, licking his paws.

Most of the people in the street have been longing to 'put him down,' which, I understand, is the expression used to describe the sinking activity of dying, and one must beware when tying a stone of lifelessness around anything to make sure one does not also attach the stone to one's own neck – they say.

No one owns the tom; he just appears, and leaves in each house a curl of black and white kittens sucking at a contented suave queen. His reproductions in color are faultless.

But I leaned out of my window. 'Scat!' I said to the tom, hissing at him. 'Go on, scat.'

He winked at me.

'First the blowfly, now me,' he said. 'If the evidence of 57 death does not satisfy you, and the evidence of life satisfies you still less, how in the world are you ever to find satisfaction?'

'Mark my words, you will go to war, my lady.'

'Certainly I will go to war,' I replied sharply.

And I shut the window and drew a boundary of war, and there I remain to this day, fighting off the armies of life and death which emerge, with the sun, from a night of frost and a morning of mist.

A Note on Janet Frame

Janet Frame, 1924–, New Zealand novelist, born in Dunedin, was brought up in Oamaru (the 'Waimaru' of her novels) on the eastern coast of South Island as a member of a poor family in a generally affluent farming area. She attended Dunedin Teachers College and Otago University and subsequently became a teacher, but left the profession within a year and earned a living looking after four elderly women in a boarding house. Her first book, *The Lagoon* (1951), a collection of short stories, was written at the age of 21. She was deeply affected by the drowning of two of her sisters in separate accidents in 1937 and 1947 and had a number of nervous breakdowns. From 1947 to 1955 she spent most of the time in psychiatric hospitals, an experience which is treated in several of her novels, where 'madness' becomes a metaphor for escape from the constrictions of society and schizophrenia is seen to involve breaking down structures which inhibit personal growth. She subsequently went overseas, spending most of 1957 in Ibiza and Andorra and subsequently living in England for seven years, an experience which is described in the third volume of her autobiography, *The Envoy from Mirror City* 59

(1985). Generally regarded as New Zealand's finest living novelist, Frame has won several awards for her fiction in her own country and in 1983 was awarded the CBE. Her first novel, *Owls Do Cry* (1957), is an account of growing up in a small New Zealand town. *Faces in the Water* (1961) describes a journey through madness. Novels like *The Edge of the Alphabet* (1962), *Scented Gardens for the Blind* (1963) and *Living in the Maniototo* (1981) are about communication and the problems of realizing experience in language, a major concern of all Frame's fiction. Set in England, *The Adaptable Man* (1965) represents a departure from her earlier work in that it deals with a larger cast of characters and appears to be more concerned with providing a picture of society, but again the novel is about alienation and the problems of conformity. *Intensive Care* (1970) and *Daughter Buffalo* (1972) grew from periods Frame spent at a writers' colony in the United States and both expose humanity's capacity for death and destruction. Frame's other novels include *A State of Siege* (1966) and *The Rainbirds* (1968), reissued as *Yellow Flowers in the Antipodean Room* (1969). She has also published three other collections of stories and sketches, a children's book and a volume of verse, *The Pocket Mirror* (1967). The three volumes of her autobiography are *To the Is-land* (1982), *An Angel at My Table* (1984), and *The Envoy from Mirror City* (1985).